NO PROOF OF MALICE

Jerry Goldberg

I0530548

FORWARD

Suppose you receive credible information that an individual is about to commit mass murder. You go to the police but due to lack of proof, they do nothing. You are 99% sure that this act will occur. What do you do? This is the dilemma facing the protagonist of this novel. If he acts by killing the individual, he will be charged with murder. If he does nothing, scores of children will be killed.

This is not just a philosophical question. It is a moral question. Do you stop this would-be murderer or do you do nothing? If you do nothing and the gruesome crime takes place, would you be willing to live with yourself? On the other hand, if you act, how would you later prove that you actually knew the crime would take place?

America has been going through a spate of school killings by deranged individuals using weapons that were designed for the military, or for the police. This novel concerns itself with two questions. One, is it right and moral to commit a crime to save many other lives and two, should America ban the sale of weapons of mass murder to help preserve a civil society?

Chapter One

It was 7:30 AM on May 23, 2013. Joe saw the boy just ahead, right on time, on his way to school. Joe approached the boy and when he was about five feet from him asked if he was Richard Kotera. The boy looked up, and said: "Yeah, who are you?"

At which time Joe removed his 22 caliber gun from his jacket, took aim and fired one shot into the boy's abdomen.

Richard fell to the ground, mortally wounded. Joe immediately took out his cell phone and dialed 911. Then he went over to the boy's body to see if he was alive. Within minutes, the police and an ambulance arrived. The EMT pronounced Richard dead on the scene. Joe had dropped the gun on the ground after the shooting so the policeman picked it up, and after questioning Joe for a few minutes, placed him in the squad car to await a police detective.

The EMT called to the policeman: "Officer, please come over here." Officer John Bailey walked the few feet to the boy's dead body and the EMT handed him a semi-automatic hand-gun and three clips of ammunition that he had just removed from the boy's jacket pockets. Bailey exclaimed: "Holy crap, what the hell is this?" The gun and ammunition were placed in a plastic evidence bag and put in the police car trunk.

Detective Robert Donovan arrived about five minutes later and was brought up to speed. When he heard the names Richard Kotera and Joseph Blandenberg, he remarked to the policeman, "Aw shit, damn it to hell." For Donovan was familiar with both parties.

Donovan asked the police officer to remove Joe from the squad car so that he could ask him a few questions but first Joe was read his Miranda rights. Joe said that he would obtain an attorney but would be happy to answer a few of Donovan's questions now.

However, because Joe said that he would get a lawyer, Donovan decided to wait before asking him a single question. At this time Joe was placed under arrest and brought to the State Police barracks in White Plains. Before Joe was placed in the holding pen at the barracks, he made a call to his son, told him what he had done, and asked him to call Jesse Graham, a New York City criminal attorney who was an old friend of Joe's when they were in the Marines.

Graham was a great defense attorney and had made a name for himself when he defended the Midtown Rapist in 2003 and the 57 Caliber Killer in 2009. Graham was in Washington DC but spoke to Joe's son and told him that he would not be able to get to see Joe until the next day. He was to instruct Joe not to say a word until he had a chance to speak to his father first. Graham said that Joe would have to spend that day, and maybe more in jail but the he would assess the situation and see if he could get Joe released on bail.

Michael Blandenberg, still in shock over what had happened, immediately got into his car and drove up to the White Plains police barracks.

Michael arrived and asked if he could see his dad. Donovan said no. The only one who will see him before us is his lawyer.

Michael begged: "Can you relay a message to him for me? Please tell him that Jesse Graham will be here tomorrow and said that he should keep his mouth shut." Donovan retorted: "I'll see what I can do."

The killing had made the 6 PM news and all channels lead with the story. "Man murders boy in cold blood." The networks sent their roving reporters to Jerusalem, New York to get as many facts as they could. This would be the media circus of the year. Even Court TV was there, getting as much dirt on Joe that it could, just in case this murder went to trial.

Joe's girlfriend Jane Willis, a professor of psychology at Moab College heard the news and went to the police. She was frantic. She begged the police to let her see Joe, but to no avail. When Michael arrived, he tried to console Jane, but then both of them started to sob.

Jane cried out: "I can't believe that he really did this. He is not a violent man. There must be a mistake." Michael said: "Let's not worry ourselves to death. This will all get sorted out. My father must have had a good reason to do what he did." Jane resumed her sobbing.

At ten o'clock the next morning, Joe was brought to the White Plains New York court house for arraignment. When he was led in, in chains, he saw his children and his old friend Jesse waiting for him at the defense table. In a few minutes, the judge arrived and the proceedings commenced. The ADA presented the preliminary findings to the court and then said that Joe was charged with 2nd degree murder.

The judge asked Joe: "How do you plead, guilty or not guilty?" Jesse shot back immediately: "Not guilty, your honor. We ask that the defendant be released on his own recognizance as he is a pillar of the community and has never been charged with a crime." The ADA shot back: "Your honor, this was a brutal murder of an innocent eighteen year old boy that had everything to live for. We ask that the defendant be held without bail."

The judge, who was up for re-election next year, and cognizant of public opinion said that bail would be set at $3 million cash or bond. As Joe was removed from the court, Jesse told him to be strong and that he would be down to see him as soon as possible.

The County jail was across the street from the court house. As Joe was being led away, the reporters shot questions at him, as they usually do in situations like this. Joe just ignored the reporters as he was led to the elevator by three correction's officers.

Jesse met with Michael and Jane in a waiting room and asked them if they could raise the bail. Michael said that his NYC condo was worth about $750,000 but that there was a mortgage on it of $300,000. "So far, not good" said Jesse.

Michael then continued: "My sister's place is worth more but she would have to ask her husband to do it as the apartment was in his name. Maybe we could raise $1 million from the two apartments. My father said that he had about $500,000 in securities and his home was worth about $300 grand. Would we be able to get a bondsman to put up the bail with these assets?"

Jesse said that it would be possible. Speak to your wife and sister and see if they have no objections. "Jane, can you help?"

Jane said that she would be of little help. She had about $50,000 in savings and she would bring it to the table. She continued: "As a full professor with tenure, the college provided me with a campus apartment and I never saved much after I got divorced from my first husband."

"Ok, there is nothing you two can do here now. Go home and I will call you with any news. I must see your dad as soon as he is processed."

As the two walked away, Jane suggested that they all use Joe's home as a main base of operations. Jane said that she would take a leave of absence for the fall term at the college. She loved Joe and wanted to support him in any way she could.

About half-an-hour later, Jesse was in the visitor's area of the jail when a guard led Joe into the room.

"Jesse, you haven't changed a bit since we last saw each other. What was that about ten years ago?"

"Yes, that's right Joe. I can't believe that we are meeting here like this. I can't believe that you could have done this. I need to know what happened and why. The police say that the gun that killed that kid was yours and that your finger prints are all over it, and the bullets inside. Tell me everything that happened, and start from the beginning. Let me power-up my I-pad."

Joe began telling his story.

Chapter Two

About nine months before

Joseph Blandenberg lived on the west side of Jerusalem, New York, a New York City suburb, about a mile and a half from Moab College, a liberal arts school. Joe was a widower, whose wife died from cancer about a year ago. He has two children, who both live in the city. Joe had recently come out of a mild depression caused by his wife's death. He was looking for a full-time teaching position.

Joe had left a government job to be at his wife's side during her final months. He had worked for the Defense Department in the Psychological Warfare Division. He had spent twenty-five years at the DOD but because he was not quite fifty-five, he could not draw down on his pension.

He wanted to teach abnormal psychology at a college where he could continue his studies about extra-sensory perception. For the DOD, he headed up a department doing research in telekinesis, mind control and other aspects of ESP. His research also included working with identical twins, telepathy, intuition and mind reading.

He was plunked out of the US Marines when he showed signs of being able to read minds and make predictions. In the nineties he worked on psychological warfare projects designed by US intelligence agencies, aimed at Russia, North Korea and Iran. However, results of these efforts were spotty at best, the Pentagon down-graded his work and reduced his department's budgets in the last three years of his government service.

Joe's wife died in 2009. After his wife passed away, Joe worked several part-time jobs that commenced in 2010 and lasted until 2012. In January 2012, Joe turned fifty-five and started to collect his $85,000 per annum pension.

Although financial pressures were no longer a problem, Joe still wanted to work a full-time job. In April, he landed a teacher's position at Moab. He replaced a teacher who died of a heart attack several weeks before. Joe was hired to complete the term. If it worked out, Joe's contract could be extended for two years.

The college was located just east of Jerusalem. The campus was just outside the city limits, about one and one-half mile from Joe's house. Joe would be an instructor in the school's psychology department and he would teach three one-hour classes and one two-hour lecture each week. For the classes, he had to basically follow the general curriculum, which was college mandated. However, for the lecture, he was given wide berth to cover other areas, and he made good use of these lectures to delve into his forte of extra-sensory perception.

In April, with the weather iffy and cool, Joe drove to the campus in his car. After a month, when the temperature moderated, Joe was able to walk or jog to and from the campus. This was no problem as he was physically-fit.

Joe was six feet, one inch tall and weighed one hundred and eighty-five pounds. He worked out five times a week and once ran a NYC marathon in three hours, fifty-two minutes. He enjoyed the exercise. It helped clear his mind.

Joe's politics were moderate. He had been a life-long Republican but lately had voted as an independent. He was an avid hunter and owned a hunting rifle and a licensed and registered 22 caliber hand-gun. The latter never left his house as it was bought strictly for home protection.

Joe was also a great reader. In fact, he was a speed reader who could read an average-sized book page in twelve seconds with full comprehension of what he had just read. This came in handy when he landed the teaching job. He needed to read and learn the course syllabus and bring himself up to where his predecessor had left off.

Faculty member, Jane Willis, a professor of psychology at the school would become Joe's mentor. She helped Joe get acclimated to the school and introduced him to the rest of the faculty. She also reviewed his class projects, lecture subjects and frequently sat in during his classes. She was forty-seven years old and attractive. She also was an avid athlete who ran three miles every day, either outside, weather permitting or on a treadmill. She also played tennis one night a week and had an eighteen handicap in golf.

Eventually, as their relationship grew, Jane invited Joe to play a round of golf at the town's semi-private golf-course. Joe's handicap was only twenty-four, so she could teach him a thing or two. Any round breaking 100 would make him very happy.

Jane was a divorcee with no children. Being free as a bird, she was able to do pretty much as she pleased in her spare time. She also had tenure which meant that for all intents and purposes she could not be fired from her job.

Joe and Jane began dating, slowly at first as Joe wanted to concentrate on doing a good job in the months left in the spring term. Besides, it was around this time that students would be getting ready for final exams, and Joe also had to prepare them and mark them. This was time consuming.

Jane had used her influence to get Joe's contract extended to cover the summer session. Accordingly, Jane canceled a planned vacation to Europe that would have lasted the entire month of July.

Joe, in his short time teaching at Moab had generated some excitement among a large number of students and his summer classes were filled to capacity. The subject of extra-sensory perception was always interesting to people as it was part of the abnormal segment of psychology. As it turned out, many of the summer students felt that they were in some way either clairvoyant or had been born with a certain gift. As the lectures were sort of a free-for-all, the "touched" students all sat up in the front rows and volunteered their psychic experiences.

One student, Cindy James was called on to tell her story and she started right in. A close friend, Etta had died last year of a rare form of breast cancer. Although Etta was only twenty, she could not fight off this virulent form of the disease. Her mother and aunt had also died from this cancer so it was no surprise that she came down with the disease. Three days after Etta was buried, Cindy's phone rang at home.

Cindy said: "I picked up the phone and said hello. I didn't know it at the time, but my mom had also picked up the receiver in a different room. The voice at the other end was that of Etta. There was no doubt in my mind. Etta kept saying "where am I, help me, Cindy help me." I kept answering her but she could not hear me. This went on for about thirty seconds. I was scared-stiff. Finally, the phone went dead and I hung up. I was pretty shaken and thought that I might be losing my mind but my mom came into my room and said that she also had heard Etta's voice. We both started to cry and hugged each other until we had regained our composure."

Joe responded: "Cindy, I've heard a number of similar stories like yours over the years. The so-called expert psychologists or psychiatrists would always claim that what you heard was either imagined, or just a case of mistaken identity. The voice at the other end must have been someone else and due to a telephone audio mal-function, or due to your then fragile emotional state, you didn't hear what you think you heard."

"But my mom heard it too!"

Joe replied agreeably: "Yes, so for you, and your mom, there is no doubt. I can't explain how or why you heard Etta's voice three days after she died, but I believe you. It does make one think, doesn't it?"

The lecture continued as Joe began speaking about predicting the future. He wasn't referring to making general predictions on economic or financial matters, or trying to guess which team would win the World Series. These would be considered informed predictions made by a knowledgeable person.

"I'm referring to making a very specific prediction of a singular event using what I would call paranormal techniques. I did a lot of work for the government in this area, and I have to admit that I have been blessed with this ability, but only in a limited way, and only on an infrequent basis. It's only happened a few times in my life. Does anyone else feel that they have this ability?"

Several students raised their hands and Joe called on Samuel Ford. Sam was twenty-six years old. He had taken several years off to travel the world and came back to school to finally earn his degree.

Sam began: "I know that I have the power of clairvoyance that we have been speaking of. I am convinced of it. Now, I haven't had any visions or anything but my predictions have amazed even myself. For instance, I would remember some insignificant fact or person from the past, and wonder why I was thinking of that. It could also have been about some song or singer or some episode of history. Then, a few days later, there would be an article or story in the newspaper or on TV about the fact or person I had been thinking of. Or it could be that this fact appeared as a clue or answer in the NY Times Crossword Puzzle. I'm sure that this has happened to everyone at some time or another. But for me, it has happened hundreds of times. I'm not exaggerating."

Joe asked the class if that experience had happened to them on many occasions and almost everyone raised their hand.

"Great, that's almost all of you. Does anyone know approximately what percentage of brain matter is actually used by most human beings on a daily basis?" Joe waited for an answer. Before anyone could speak, he told them that it was less than ten percent.

"Now, it's very possible that someone with ESP is using parts of the brain not used by almost everyone else."

"Mr. Ford, do you have any other specific predictions that you may have divined?" Joe said with a big smile on his face. Sam replied: "Yes. I am an avid football fan. I watch every game I can each weekend and I am very knowledgeable of all sorts of football statistics. In January 2006, I, along with my brother and three friends were watching a game between the New England Patriots and the Miami Dolphins. Prior to the game starting, I predicted that quarterback Doug Flute would make a successful drop kick extra-point at some time during the game.

Usually, after a touchdown is made, the team uses its place-kicker to score the extra point. Now early in the history of the sport, way back in the 1900s, the extra point was made when someone converted a successful drop-kick. However, the drop-kick went out of fashion many years ago and was no longer used. When I made this prediction, my friends looked perplexed, and all asked me what a drop-kick was. They had never heard of it.

They all thought I was nuts until Flute actually made the kick late in the fourth quarter of the game. It was the first drop kick made since 1941."

"Very interesting" said Joe. "Could you have heard a sportscast in the days prior to the game when someone may have said that Flute was considering trying this play? Couldn't you have heard it and maybe it went into your sub-conscience?"

Sam replied: "Impossible because in the week prior to the game, I spent five days in Aruba on winter vacation and did not read a single thing, other than a menu, or watch any TV or listen to any radio that entire time."

The lecture continued for another hour or so, and student after student told their stories, and explaining that they took this course because they were looking for answers.

The summer was soon over. Joe and Jane, as their relationship had advanced to a higher level, took a few days to visit the city to take in a few Broadway shows and eat that some fine restaurants. As Jane had sat in on some of Joe's lectures, she was able to discuss the many stories she had heard from the students. Jane was no acolyte of the paranormal. All of the experiences could be explained as coincidence, educated guesses, luck or just vivid imaginations.

However, she was a scientist and therefore open to all possibilities. She told Joe that sitting in on the lectures was in some way similar to watching the Twilight Zone on TV. She was, however, very happy for Joe's immediate success, as his classes were full, his students were enthused and none of them ever missed a lecture.

Chapter Three

It was the first day of school at JFK High School in Jerusalem, New York. Richard Kotera dreaded this day. He was now a senior and had spent two miserable years in this school, subject to incessant abuse, both physical and psychological. The bullying had started in elementary school.

Richard had always been rather slight of build, so at first, the abuse was verbal. They called him the skinny runt. The verbal insults never ceased and after a few years, his personality had changed.

He was born normal and had a happy family life for his first five years. He was the only child of Sharon and Burt Kotera. His parents had wanted more children, but Sharon had miscarried three times, once prior to Richard's birth and twice thereafter. Had his parents had more children, maybe things would have been different for Richard.

Not known to either Richard or his mom, Burt became unhappy in the marriage and one day when Richard was six, his father left the home, and asked Sharon for a divorce. Richard was too young to understand that he was not the cause of his father's discontent, but nevertheless blamed himself when his father left. Every boy needs a father and Richard was no different. Richard's future was now set in stone.

With the constant bullying at school, and no father figure at home, Richard was a lost soul. His mother was no help in the years after Burt left. She herself had gone into a deep funk and required anti-depression medicine.

The personality changes were at fist subtle but soon Richard became a loner. He had tried to make friends but could not and he didn't understand why. Perhaps it was his physical stature, or lack thereof. At some point he stopped trying and for the next ten years, never had a single friend.

Jerusalem was a small hamlet, about forty miles from New York City. The population was about 5,000. There was only one elementary school, one middle school and one high school. As a result, everyone knew everyone else, and Richard would be trapped in his own private hell for these ten years.

His arch-nemesis was Tim McMahon, a tall boy at seven who would eventually develop into a rather large athletic type. He was good in sports, but feared by other students, rather than liked or respected. Tim was the oldest of four brothers. His father was a CPA who had his own practice.

Unfortunately for the McMahon brothers, their father was a heavy drinker who physically abused his sons. As a result, Tim, himself became an abuser, always starting fights with other boys. Richard was easy picking for Tim. Tim would force Richard to turn over his lunch money, threatening to beat Richard up if he did not comply. This happened almost every day and Richard never told a soul.

The abuse continued through middle school. Although Richard was in constant fear of Tim, he rationalized that it must be his fault. So when Tim would slap the back of Richard's head, Richard would apologize. It made no sense to Tim but he liked the idea, so the slapping would continue until the assistant principal witnessed one incident. Fearing retribution, Richard told the assistant principal that this was a single occurrence and that he had started the altercation with Tim.

Soon thereafter, Tim got other boys to join in the bullying. Some of them went along out of fear for Tim but a few were just like Tim and enjoyed making Richard's life miserable. Some of the teachers at the school had a feeling that something was wrong and tried to intervene, but Richard always said that nothing was wrong, and that no one was bullying him.

He was an extreme introvert. Without friends, he never participated in the classroom or in any extra-curricular activities. He hardly ever spoke to anyone. However, he did enough studying of his subjects to get reasonably good marks on his tests, and received grades between B and B+.

After school, he would hurry home and go right into his room and surf the internet. His favorite sites included those dealing with Satan and the black arts, violent video games, guns and ammunition and chat rooms with other like-minded people. His computer was password protected to make sure that his mother or anyone else would not be able to access his favorite sites.

At 8 AM, Richard was sitting in homeroom with his classmates waiting for his teacher. While all others were conversing or laughing, Richard was staring out of the window. He could hear several of his classmates whispering, and he was sure they were talking about him. He couldn't make out exactly what was being said but he did hear word like screwball, maniac and nutcase. They were snickering as they spoke and were glancing at him. This was a typical morning for Richard at JFK.

The rest of this day was rather uneventful which was a surprise to him until he realized that he hadn't crossed paths with Tim or any of his minions. At 3:30 he entered his room and went directly to his computer. Going on-line transported him to his own fantasy world.

He was a frequent participant of a web-based chat room named "The Legions of Lucifer." He began chatting with Jack Clifton, a Pasadena, California teenager who was suffering a similar life experience in his home town.

Jack wrote that he was almost at his breaking point and was going to strike back at his enemies. When Richard asked how, Jason said that maybe he would throw acid in the faces of his tormentors, blinding them, or maybe just stabbing them with scissors in the gym locker room when they weren't looking.

Richard had thought of retaliation but never in a serious way. Now, after listening to Jack, he imagined what it would feel like if he struck back at Tim and the rest. How would I do it, he thought? Maybe I would use acid, like Jack, or maybe I would use a gun to blow all of them away. In any case, he thought about what to do for hours at a time over the next few weeks.

At this point, his school work started to suffer and he was failing his tests on a regular basis. His mom was called in to school for meetings with the school's guidance counselor. In addition to Richard's poor performance, the counselor discussed the possibility that Richard might need a psychiatrist. His usual odd behavior had gotten even odder. The counselor thought that Richard might eventually do harm to himself, or to others.

His mother thought that the school was over-reacting. After all, Richard had never started a fight or made verbal threats against anyone. Maybe he was just odd. There was no law against that. Sharon promised to work with her son after school and on weekends and try to get him to open up. If necessary, she would seek the help of a mental health professional, but right now, she didn't think that her son was in any real trouble.

After several of these meetings, Richard was now convinced that even the school officials were against him. He would soon get even with everyone.

Chapter Four

It was Christmas day. Joe's two children were visiting their dad. Jane was there to meet Joe's family. His son, Michael came along with his wife Karen and their two children. His daughter, Laurie arrived shortly after with her husband Bob and their two kids.

The school year was almost half over. Michael asked his dad how things were going. Joe started to tell his son about all of his gifted students. Michael listened but with a skeptical frown on his face. Michael had his doubts about ESP and for the most part, thought it was mumbo-jumbo. Joe continued to speak when Michael interrupted: "Jane, what is your opinion of my father's theories?"

Jane replied: "Well, it's not my field of training and while I am somewhat skeptical I have sat in on some your dad's lectures. These lectures are inter-active. I mean that he just doesn't talk for two hours, but allows the students to tell their experiences, and to elicit comments from them.

Some of these stories are fantastic. I teach Psych 1, 2 and 3. The latter course is advanced Psych and includes aspects of abnormal psychology. These areas include the study of various psychoses, schizophrenia, paranoia, neuroses and other forms of brain disorders. Most of these can be treated with medications. This is science, this is medicine.

However, as far as your dad's theories are concerned, I believe that anything is possible, and I have an open mind."

During dinner, the assemblage was conversing around the table when all of a sudden Joe, who had been quiet for a while exclaimed: "Michael, I just got a strange thought. Not a vision, mind you, but a strong feeling that you have just landed a new job and would be working for the Medallion Bank in lower Manhattan. Your salary will double from what it was at Harrison Bank, and you would be a senior vice president. Has my imagination run wild or something? Tell me I'm nuts."

Michael and Karen were looking at each other in amazement. Michael had, in fact, just accepted a new job precisely as his father had stated. Michael had only heard back from his new employer the day before and the only other person with this knowledge was Karen.

Michael then said: "Karen, you told him, didn't you?'

Karen replied: "Absolutely not."

Michael seemed not to believe her so she swore this on their children's lives. There was no way Karen would lie about this, and Michael looked at his dad and asked him: "How?"

Joe replied: "Were you thinking about any of this just before I said it?"

"Yes" said Michael.

"Then it makes sense, but only if you believe that I have this ability. These thoughts had just come into my head seconds before I blurted them out."

"Dad, maybe you are not as crazy as I thought" Michael said laughingly.

At this point Laurie chimed in: "Dad, from 1 to 100, what number am I thinking of right now?" It was, of course a joke but Joe played along. He made a face as if he had put himself in a trance and after about fifteen seconds said: "I have no idea, who do you think I am, Houdini?" Everyone laughed.

"Actually", Joe said, "my gift if you can call it that comes and goes, transient, so to speak. I haven't had a vibe like this for months. I would never claim that I could read minds. I don't want to be besieged by the curious, or by people who would want me to contact their dearly departed. In fact, I am at a loss to explain it other than to say that I do have this extra sensory perception. I certainly would not have worked in this field if I had thought otherwise."

Bob whimsically asked Joe to predict what stocks would double in the next year. He continued: "I need to keep your daughter in the lifestyle that she has become accustomed to." Everyone laughed and the conversation continued for a while before they all went into the den. The grandchildren were playing with toys while the adults watched some Christmas movie on cable. It was a good Christmas.

Jane liked Joe's family and made sure that she told them that by the end of the evening. As it turned out, the feelings were mutual. The kids liked the idea that Joe was seeing a mature, intelligent woman and not a twenty-five year old groupie-type nymph. That would not have been respectful to the memory of their deceased mother.

Later, Joe's family left to return to the city as Tuesday was a work day. Joe and Jane watched them leave from the front door. Joe put his arm around Jane and they went inside.

A week later, with winter break over, unseasonably warm weather hit the northeast and the temperature went to the upper sixties. That allowed Joe the opportunity to jog to Moab. On Tuesday January 4th, Joe had almost made it to Jerusalem city limit when he slowed down to a walk. As he passed the corner of Jeret Drive and Walker Street he almost collided with a student on his way to school. The student had been walking with his head down and wearing a jacket with a hoody. This guy wasn't looking where he was going.

Joe yelled: "Excuse me." The young man ignored him. The near collision was the complete fault of this kid and he refused to acknowledge anything. The boy continued down the block without saying a word or looking back. As Joe continued to watch him, he suddenly had a bad feeling, a sort of dread about this miscreant. He couldn't put his finger on it, but something wasn't right. This was Joe's first encounter with Richard Kotera, but it wouldn't be his last.

Chapter Five

For the next few days, Joe continued to think about his encounter with that boy. It wasn't just that he may have been different or weird, but he was emitting a negativity that Joe couldn't explain. It was palpable and Joe couldn't ignore it. Joe decided that it would be wise to walk to work over the next few days and hope that he would encounter this boy again. If Joe was wrong, and there was nothing to worry about he wanted to know this as soon as possible.

With the episode at home during Christmas dinner and this chance meeting with the boy, Joe's long-dormant powers may have returned. Joe had not been fully truthful with his family. When the powers returned, they could last for days at a time and were not as transient as he made them out to be.

One evening four months later, Richard chatted with Jack for over two hours. He was quickly zoning out of reality. The conversation was entirely about how Richard was going to crush his enemies. Jack had chickened out and had not done anything to his tormentors. But he was very enthusiastic about how to help Richard. He was egging him on, but in a subtle way. It wouldn't take much to bring Richard to the edge of the cliff. He would do something soon.

There was a knock on his bedroom door. It was his mother. Richard ended his chat with Jack and shut down his computer.

"Richard, come down stairs, I need to talk with you."

Richard sat down opposite his mom at the kitchen table and said "What's up?"

"Well, the bastard who calls himself your father stopped paying alimony and child support about two weeks ago. I just found out that he left his apartment and disappeared with a girlfriend. I spoke with his lawyer and even he doesn't know how to reach him. It looks like he is trying to avoid paying us any more money which means that paying for college will be difficult or impossible. Also, with my income, we won't be able to afford this house anymore. The bank will eventually foreclose on the mortgage. We're screwed, Rich."

Sharon kept speaking about their predicament. Richard listened without saying a word. Later, back in his room, Richard added his father to the list of who should die when he would seek revenge. He kept repeating to himself, "that bastard, that bastard." This was the straw that broke the camel's back.

Richard started to make plans. He decided to use a gun. He would need it to be a rapid fire gun. He went on line and did research. It looked like the Glock-31 357 magnum semi-automatic pistol would do just fine. It had a clip of fourteen bullets that could be fired in about fifteen seconds.

Richard had to figure out how to procure this weapon. The next day Jack told him that there was a loophole in the gun laws that might allow him to buy a gun at a gun show. The dealers at these shows would sell a gun to Charles Manson, if given the chance. All he had to do was to show a driver's license or other proof of age, and prove that he was at least eighteen. There would be no background check of any kind.

Joe surfed until he found what he was looking for. In three days, there would be a gun show in Wayne, New Jersey. Since the show was on a Saturday, Richard was able to borrow his mom's car and travel to it.

He purchased the Glock semi for $500 plus a dozen clips of ammo for another $100. The dealer put the gun and ammunition in a plain brown bag. Richard left the show and drove home in about two hours.

After returning, Richard contacted Jack and filled him in. Jack gave Richard instructions on what to do next. He was to draw out a map of the school listing its entrances and exits. He needed to know where and when to strike. "Where would Tim be at the precise time?" He should be the first to go, when the time came.

Richard spent the rest of the weekend making plans, drawings and lists of his enemies. After careful thought, Richard decided that he would do the deed on graduation day, about a month from now. The entire senior class would be there, and they would be crowded together in the gymnasium.

Chapter Six

Joe walked to work every day for almost three months after first coming upon the strange boy. He once followed him back to his house one afternoon and discovered his identity, Richard Kotera, an only son to Sharon Kotera. However, Joe felt no vibe as he had almost a month before. Finally, two days before the high school graduation, Joe passed Richard on the street precisely where they had their first encounter.

This time, Joe picked up the seething anger inside this boys mind, and was able to determine that Richard was planning a mass murder at the school, two days later. Joe started to panic. He wasn't sure what to do. "Jane will know" he said to himself.

Once at Moab, Joe went right to Jane who was conducting her first class of the day. He called her outside of the classroom and said he needed her immediately, for something. She calmed him down and said that she would see him after the class was over. Later, he told her of his encounters with Richard and what the boy was planning two days later. She asked him if he was absolutely sure.

"Jane, it's not an absolute science. I can't be 100% sure, but I know what I heard. It was as clear as day. I'm as sure as I can be."

Jane replied: "Let's go to the police right now. I'll go with you"

"They'll think I'm nuts Jane."

"No, here is what you will say." Jane gave him the story line that might make his charges believable. About an hour later, the two of them arrived at the Jerusalem Police Station and asked for a detective. After a few minutes, they were led into the office of Robert Donovan.

"How can I help you?"

Joe replied: "Well, I have information that a high school student, one Richard Kotera is planning a mass school shooting in two days at JFK High School."

"How do you know this?"

"I received a tip from another student who knows this Kotera boy."

"What's his name?" asked Donovan.

"I'd rather not say at this time. I gave this person my word that I would keep him, out of it. He fears for his life, you know, from this Kotera boy."

"Do you know where Kotera lives?" asked Donovan.

"Yes, 1315 Walker Street, here in town."

"Well, I don't know what I can do about this. You say you got a tip but cannot give me the name of the informant. You don't seem to have any proof that this boy will do anything. How can I proceed without anything to go on?"

Joe then started yelling: "I'm as positive as I could be that this boy will kill dozens of students in two days and you won't lift a finger to help. What kind of a cop are you?"

Donovan shot back: "Now, get a hold of yourself and calm yourself down. Ok, I'll go to this kid's home, speak to him or his mother and check him out at the school."

"When will you go?"

"Tomorrow, first thing, I promise."

As Joe and Jane walked away, Donovan thought to himself: "what a nut job." However, he promised to follow-up, however perfunctorily.

The two of them drove away. Joe said: "What an ass. Did you see how he looked at me? He thought I was crazy. Could you imagine what his reaction would have been if I told him the truth? I mean, exactly how I came upon this information. He's not going to do anything, that moron."

Jane said: "He said that he would, now let the police handle it. Please don't do anything foolish. Remember, you said that this wasn't an exact science. If you are 99% sure means that there is still a 1% chance you could be wrong."

"OK, OK, I'll let Donovan handle it, but I will call him tomorrow to make sure."

The next day, Joe called Detective Donovan at 10 AM. The detective was not in but the message was passed along to him from dispatch. Donovan called Joe's cell number and the two spoke.

Donovan spoke: "Nothing yet, I went to the boy's home at 8:30 AM. No one was home. The mother must work and the boy must have gone to school. So, I went to the school and spoke to the principal. This guy wasn't too helpful citing privacy issues. I told him that we had gotten a tip that Kotera was going to shoot up the school tomorrow and the guy opened up a little.

He told me that the kid was from a broken home and had no friends that anyone knew of. He was a loner and no one knew much about him. That scared me a little, I must admit. These are the types of kids that will do a mass shooting. So at this time, I don't have much but I will visit the home again early this evening and make sure I speak to the kid and his mother. I'll call you later tonight."

Joe felt a slight sigh of relief as it seemed that Donovan was starting to worry, and was taking this seriously.

Jane spent the evening at Joe's house and they both waited for Donovan's call. It never came. That evening, there was a robbery at Clancy's, a bar on Main St. and the bartender was shot. Donovan was the lead investigator. He totally forgot to call Joe as this was a real-life crime and not a possible one in the future.

For the next two hours, Joe and Jane talked about what to do. Jane made him promise that he himself would do nothing, and they would hope for the best. As Jane had to give one last final exam the next day, she left Joe's house and headed for her campus apartment.

Chapter Seven

Two days after the shooting, the NY City media left Jerusalem and the story got old. Due to the mounting legal costs, Joe could not make bail and was in jail for the next five months. That would make it difficult to come up with a proper defense. Jesse Graham had to make weekly visits to the jail to interview Joe and strategize.

The District Attorney's office was building its case slowly. At first, it believed that its case would be a slam-dunk. After-all, it had Joe's gun, the bullets, all with Joe's finger prints on them. Donovan would give testimony that Joe came to him just two days before the shooting with his fantastic story, and the prosecution was ready to call Jane to the stand as a hostile witness, if necessary.

However, the prosecutors would have trouble explaining Kotera's semi-automatic gun and clips of bullets found on him after the shooting. The DA's office had interviewed dozens of students and found that Richard's behavior matched the profile of a school shooter.

Assistant District Attorney Barbara Smith, a prosecuting attorney with fifteen years experience was assigned the case. She was the best prosecutor in the White Plains office having spent ten years working in the New York City District Attorney's office. Richard's computer was confiscated as evidence but no incriminating evidence was found on it.

During discovery, the prosecutor had to turn over all evidence collected against Joe. This included physical evidence, ballistics, the 911 call and interviews with all potential witnesses. Since information from the computer was non-existent, it was not turned over to the defense.

On August 31st, the Westchester County District Attorney James Matheson announced that the trial of Joseph Blandenberg would commence on October 3rd and that the prosecuting team would be led by Barbara Smith, a person well known in Westchester County. Judge Robin Grobin would preside over the case.

The media interest in the case started up again. Carter's Court televised a one ½ hour special on the case that evening. Host Jeanne Carter, who never met a defendant she didn't despise, was already rousing the rabble, convicting Joe even before the trial started. It looked like there would be a media circus after all.

Jesse met with Joe in a visitor's room on September 12th to go over the defense strategy.

Jesse started in: "The DA still has not released the kid's computer to us for inspection. I will subpoena it. I think that there must be something incriminating on it that Smith doesn't want us to see. And, if we find that she was withholding exculpatory evidence, we can get public opinion on our side, plus get her sanctioned by the bar."

Joe didn't really care. He knew what he knew, and even if he was found guilty, it would not matter that much to him. He saved countless lives that day.

Jesse: "Joe, we need a better defense than: I read his mind and that's why I killed him. Now, if you could prove that you have extra-sensory perception while on the witness stand…..well, then maybe we have a chance."

"Jesse, I haven't had those feelings since the day of the shooting. They're gone. I couldn't predict the weather even if I was outside, and it was raining cats and dogs. I don't know if I will ever have the ability again. It's as if God took it away as punishment for what I did."

"OK, Joe, let's go over the time-line once more. I want to make sure that you haven't left anything out. Back in early January, you were walking to Moab, right? Continue."

Joe repeated the facts to Jesse, as he had done at least six times before. There was no change in his story.

"OK Joe, I've got it. With the evidence against you, I may have to put you on the stand. I rarely do that, but in this case, it may be our best chance to explain your actions, and maybe convince a few jurors that what you did wasn't murder.

The next day, Jesse filed his subpoena to obtain Richard's computer. Barbara Smith strenuously objected. The judge admonished her. "You know the rules of evidence Barbara, growled Judge Grobin. Smith tried to explain: We are afraid that if we turn over the computer, the defense may accidentally destroy the contents, even though there is nothing exculpatory in them.

After the two lawyers argued for about three minutes, the judge offered a compromise. "You will turn over the computer to the FBI lab in Quantico, and the defense will give the FBI a list of what it is looking for, if anything." The two attorneys both nodded in agreement. The judge shot back: "Now if this analysis takes longer than, say one month, I will have to postpone the trial accordingly."

Jesse took this compromise as a small victory. He not only got the judge to agree to the subpoena but got him to admonish the prosecutor for her conduct regarding the computer contents.

The next few weeks went by too fast, and the trial was looming over Joe like a heavy tarp. He was scared, but still sure that his actions were correct, even heroic. However, he knew that it would be an uphill battle to avoid a life sentence. Jeanne Carter, a prosecutor's best friend was ready, and this worried Jesse to no end. He needed public opinion to be on Joe's side, or at least to be neutral.

Chapter Eight

The trial started, right on time with jury selection. All of the proceedings were being televised on Court TV. The selection took two days and Jesse seemed to be satisfied with it. There were eight women and four men. Jesse wanted as many women on the jury as possible. If he could persuade the jury that Kotera was about to commit mass murder, women would be more sympathetic to a man, whose actions may have saved children's lives.

At least, that was Jesse's theory. The country had seen too many mass killings by students. He would remind them of Newtown, Columbine, and Virginia Tech during the trial.

The court was filled to capacity with Joe's family, students and other supporters as well as reporters, court room groupies and the general public. Each day of the trial, with the exception for the family, the seats would be given out using a lottery system.

Prosecutor Smith gave her opening statement. Joe was watching the proceedings but didn't really hear the words. Months in jail had taken their toll on him. It was, in a way surreal. From time to time, he would focus and actually hear some of Smith's statement.

"The State will prove that the defendant, Joseph Blandenberg, shot and killed Richard Kotera, an eighteen year old teenager in cold blood, for no obvious reason. What he committed was murder, pure and simple."

Ms. Smith's opening statement lasted for ½ hour and by the time it was over, the jury looked like it wanted to drag Joe out of the court room and hang him without hearing his defense.

The judge then pointed to Jesse: "Mr. Graham, your turn."

Jesse got up and walked to the microphone, faced the jury and began his opening statement.

"The prosecutor, in her opening statement has stated that my client, the defendant, murdered Richard Kotera in cold blood, with malice and without any mitigating circumstances. We intend to prove, however, that Joe Blandenberg, a pillar of the community, a man never in trouble with the law, a former federal employee and US Marine, is not a murderer; That Mr. Kotera, a mentally sick man was intending to commit a horrific act of mass murder of students at his high school, and had to be stopped.

How did we all feel while watching the aftermath of Newtown, Connecticut, and all the other school killings that have occurred over the last ten years or so? Think about it; Dozens of children killed by a deranged student, or students, without warning, or with obvious warning signs that were ignored. With obvious warning signs that were ignored" he repeated.

"We will show that Richard Kotera was a very troubled man who had no friends. He hardly said a word to anyone he ever came upon, never participated in any intercourse with his fellow students or teachers. He was a typical sociopath, with extreme paranoia, who eventually turned into a psychopath. We will clearly prove this beyond a shadow of a doubt.

We will show that the prosecutor's case is weak and that she ignored the obvious in her zeal to over-charge my client, and make a name for herself."

Jesse's opening statement lasted for over an hour. By the time it was done, the judge recessed the trial until the next day when Smith would call her first witness.

Jeanne Carter of Carter's Court had as her guests, Renee James, the famous defense attorney and Cleveland Stokes, famed prosecutor of many murder cases in New York. Carter asked each of them what they thought after the first day of the trial.

Renee replied first: "There's not much to report. These were only the opening statements and we have to wait until the prosecution presents its case witness by witness, exhibit by exhibit."

Cleveland chimed in: "I agree, but Jesse's opening statement was a pretty strong rebuttal of Smith's. He's really gone out on a limb there, and if he doesn't have anything to present that really disproves the prosecutor's case, Blandenberg will be sunk."

Jeanne Carter then made her first comments on the case.

"What we have here is a case of a cruel man who obviously lost his mind, deranged, who murdered a child for no apparent reason. The boy was a little odd but that's no excuse to kill him. You know, some kids develop later than usual. Who's to say that Richard Kotera would not have grown up to be a wonderful person? On the other hand, it looks like Blandenberg is the one who flipped his lid."

Jeanne spoke with her patented Alabama twang which made her both loved and hated at the same time. They loved her in the south but hated her north of the Mason-Dixon Line. She was a prosecutor's dream but the bane of all defendants.

The commentary went on for about fifteen minutes until the subject turned to another murder case from Los Angeles California.

That afternoon, Jesse visited his client in the county jail to go over the first day of the trial. Jesse then got into what would occur the next day. "Tomorrow, the DA will start calling her witnesses. First she will call the 911 telephone operator and she will offer to play the recording of your call.

That will be followed by the testimony of the police. This is all routine. I don't expect to challenge these witnesses unless I feel their testimonies are biased or in error. I have to ask you, are you having any ESP feelings?'

That's the question that Jesse had been asking Joe every time they met. "When it's our turn we will call as witnesses, your government colleagues, some of your students and Jane. But their testimony will be discounted or not believed by most of the jurors.

To most people, ESP is not real. It's just something one sees on television. It makes for a good novel, but it's not real." If you could prove that you have the power during the trial we have a great chance of winning this case."

Joe replied as he had done for the past months, "No, nada, nothing. Don't you think I would have said something to you if I'd felt it."

"Well, OK, but if you feel anything, let me know. I spoke to Jane earlier before the opening statements. She still wants to marry you."

Jane had proposed this to Joe after his indictment. A wife could not be compelled to testify against her husband. But to Joe, this looked like a stunt that would make him look guilty. He repeatedly refused Jane's proposal for that reason.

Jesse added: "Jane honestly loves you very much and I told her that even if she married you, I still needed her to testify on your behalf. At this time, she is the best witness you have. She is a respected professor at the local college, well known in Westchester County and respected by her peers. She will corroborate that she witnessed at least one episode of your perception abilities."

Day Two of the Trial-

Prosecutor Smith called Sarah Price. Sarah Price rose from her seat and entered the witness box. She put her left hand on the bible and raised her right hand, repeating the oath not to lie on the stand.

"Ms. Price, could you tell the court what your job is?'

Sarah responded: "I work as a civilian for the White Plains Police Department. I am a 911 operator."

"Ms. Price, can you tell the court about a 911 call you received on May 23, 2013 at around 7:30 in the morning?"

Price continued: "Yes, I received a call from a man who said that he had just shot a boy. I asked him to give me an address. He said Walker Street in Jerusalem New York. I asked him to repeat everything he had just said, which he did. I then asked him to give me his name, and he said Joseph Blandenberg. I asked him for his address, and he gave it to me. I know from his telephone number that he was calling from a cell phone, so I asked him not to shut it off after he completed his call, and he agreed."

ADA Smith asked her: "Why did you ask him not to shut his phone?"

"I wanted to make sure the police could track him, just in case he was incorrect about the address. Sometimes in moments of stress, a person will misspeak accidentally."

"Your honor, at this time I would like to enter into evidence as Exhibit 1, the audio recording of the 911 call, and would like to play it for the court."

The judge looked at Jesse. "No objections your honor."

The recording played exactly like Ms. Price described, except that Joe's voice indicated extreme excitement, almost to a point of incoherence. It showed that Joe may not have been the cold-blooded killer the prosecution made him out to be. Ms. Smith had a few more questions for the witness before turning her over to the defense.

Jesse stood up and said that he had no questions for the witness at this time.

The prosecutor then called Officer Bailey to the stand. After asking some questions about how many years the officer had been on the job, and what his rank was, the real questioning began. "Officer Bailey, please describe the events of May 23, 2013 as relating to this case."

Bailey answered: "I received a call from the Westchester County 911 dispatcher that a shooting had taken place on Walker Street in Jerusalem. I got there in about five minutes." Bailey started to cough. Ms. Smith asked him to continue.

"When I got to the location, the ambulance had already gotten there. I observed from my car, a man sitting on the pavement along-side a motionless body. The EMT was kneeling over the body. I later discovered that the body was that of Richard Kotera.

I asked the man for his name, and he gave it to me as Joe Blandenberg. I asked him not to get up but to put his hands behind him. I noticed a hand gun on the pavement next to him. I picked it up and placed it into an evidence bag and put it in the car's trunk."

"What happened then?"

"I got on the radio and asked for a detective to come to the scene."

"Why is that?"

"I'm only a patrolman. Investigating situations like that require that a detective be assigned. I waited for the detective."

"How long did that take?"

"Approximately ten minutes."

"Did you ask Mr. Blandenberg any questions?"

"Yes, I asked him if he knew what had happened. He was mumbling. I repeated the question. I also asked him if the gun was his. He said that it was. At that point I decided to stop the questions and wait for the detective."

The questioning of Bailey continued for about ten minutes longer. At that point, Ms. Smith looked at Jesse and said "your witness."

Jesse approached the microphone and started to speak. "Officer Bailey, did you take into custody anything else besides the hand gun?"

Bailey replied: "Yes."

"Could you describe what it was?"

"Yes, while the EMT was working on the boy's body, he removed a semi-automatic hand gun and three clips of ammunition from the boy's coat pockets. The EMT handed me the gun and ammo, and I placed those in my squad car to give to the detective."

Jesse then asked: "Did that discovery surprise you?"

"You bet it did. I was wondering what a young kid would be doing with the weapon and the bullets."

"Officer, how many bullets did each clip have in them?"

"It is my understanding that each clip had fourteen bullets."

"Was the gun already loaded?"

Bailey replied: "From what I learned back at the police barracks, yes it was, with a full clip."

Jesse then asked: "So that's a total of fifty-six possible shots to be taken, right?" The question was rhetorical, and the patrolman did not answer. "No more questions at this time."

The defense questions had certainly scored some points in the court of public opinion, and maybe with the jurors too.

The next witness to be called was Lieutenant Detective Robert Donovan. The detective's testimony lasted throughout the day. He recited the facts as he knew them, starting with Joe's visit two days prior to the killing. When it was Jesse's turn to question him, he started by asking about Donovan's past experience.

"I've been a cop for twenty-seven years."

Jesse next asked: "Detective, could you please go through your work experience before you joined the Westchester County Police Department?"

Donovan replied: "OK. After graduating the NY City Police Academy, I joined the NYPD as a foot patrolman. I served twelve years in the city."

"Did you see many murders, or other gruesome crimes while working in New York?"

"Yes, of course, dozens. That was the main reason I made the transfer to Westchester as soon as I could. It's hard to live a normal life when you have seen what I've seen."

Jesse then said: How does this killing compare with others you have seen? I mean in the ferocity or gruesomeness?"

Donovan answered: "On a 1 to 10 scale, this would be a 2, ten being the most horrid murder you could imagine."

"Thank you detective. Now let me ask you about the gun.

What kind of gun was it?"

"It was a 22 caliber Colt."

Jesse countered: "A 22, is that a powerful weapon? I mean as compared to the guns that are out there?

Donovan replied: "No, it's a rather weak pistol and rather small"

"Is it the kind of weapon that you would take with you if you intended to kill someone?"

Donovan replied: "Probably not, it doesn't have the fire power that, say, a 38 or a 44 caliber gun has."

Jesse then added: "In your vast experience as a policemen and detective, in percentage terms say, how often would a person, shot with a 22 caliber gun have been killed vs. only being wounded by the shot?"

"I'm not quite sure I understand the question."

"OK, what's the survival rate after being shot once with a 22 caliber gun, I mean based on your experience and knowledge?"

Donovan thought about it for a moment and then said: "Maybe eighty percent."

Smith jumped to her feet and objected on the basis that the question called for an opinion.

The judge over-ruled the objection.

The questioning of Detective Donovan continued until 4:30 PM at which time the judge adjourned the trial.

"We'll reconvene tomorrow at 10 AM. Detective, you will have to come back. Mr. Martin has more questions for you and you will still be under oath."

Chapter Nine

Jesse met Joe in the jail's private visitor's center to go over the day's testimony. Jesse said: "I think we scored some points about your gun. I'm hoping that the jury will see that your actions were to just stop Kotera, not necessarily kill him.

And, did you see the faces on some of the jurors when Bailey testified about the Glock automatic and the three clips of bullets? Some of them appeared to be incredulous. They must be asking why an eighteen year old student was heading to school with such an arsenal."

"Who is scheduled to testify tomorrow?" asked Joe.

"After I finish with Donovan, the prosecution will call the coroner. He will describe the nature of the wound. It should all scientific evidence and such. I will have some questions for him too.

After that, Smith will call Sharon Kotera. When it's my turn to cross, I will have to be careful not to come across as a bully, or be insensitive. But I will question her because I believe that she bears some blame in all this in not getting her kid the professional help he needed."

Day three of the trial-

The trial resumed the next morning. Jesse continued his questioning of Detective Donovan.

Jesse started right in where he had left off: "Detective isn't it so that Mr. Blandenberg and Jane Willis came to your office at the police station two days before the shooting?"

"Yes."

"Could you tell the court exactly what Mr. Blandenberg told you, and then asked you to do?"

Donovan responded: "Yes, the defendant came to my office to inform me that he felt that Richard Kotera, the deceased, was going to do a mass shooting at his high school two days later." When I asked him how he came upon this information, he said that he was given a tip by another student who he refused to name."

"Do you know why he refused to name that student?" asked Jesse.

"According to Mr. Blandenberg, this student feared for his life and he, the defendant promised to not reveal his identity."

"Did you believe him?" asked Jesse.

"Yes, I did but I told him that without the tipsters name and the lack of other evidence, there was little I could do."

"What happened next?"

"Well, Mr. Blandenberg almost went ballistic on me for not being so helpful, I suppose. At that time I told him that I would visit the boy's home and speak to him and his mother."

"Did you follow up as promised?"

"Yes, I did, but no one was home so I never interviewed anyone there. I did go to the school, JFK High School to be precise, and spoke to the principal, Mr. Stanton."

"What did you learn from Mr. Stanton?" Asked Jesse.

"At first he was reluctant to answer my questions citing student confidentiality. But after explaining why I was there, Mr. Stanton told me that Richard was a loner, an introvert, and a very strange boy. As far as Stanton knew, Richard did not have a single friend, nor did he ever participate in any school activities. I asked him if Richard had ever made any threats to the school, or to any student. Stanton said none that he was aware of."

"Did you speak to Joe; I mean the defendant later and tell him what you found out?

"Yes, I did."

Jesse then asked: "did you promise to go back to the Kotera residence that evening and speak to the boy and his mother?"

"Yes I did" Donovan paused for a few seconds and then finished his sentence: "but I never got a chance to do that because there was a robbery shooting at a bar in town that evening and the bartender was seriously wounded. There was so much excitement that I forgot to go to the Kotera residence. The on-site investigation lasted three hours."

Jesse responded: "knowing what you now know, do you regret not following up with that visit?"

Donovan hesitated but reluctantly said "yes."

Jesse said: "I'm finished with this witness."

The prosecution next called the coroner, Dr. Melvin Spearling. After going through a series of questions that confirmed his expertise, Ms. Smith asked him: "What was the exact cause of death?"

Spearling answered: "Death was caused by a single gun shot wound to the abdomen that pierced Mr. Kotera's liver, pancreas and spleen causing massive blood loss along with the trauma. Mr. Kotera went into shock and was dead within ten minutes."

Smith replied: "What else did your autopsy find?"

"Well, I removed a 22 caliber bullet from his body. I gave the bullet, which was in good shape, to forensics. The gun expert compared that bullet with the gun found at the scene."

"And, what were the results?"

"The bullet that we removed from Mr. Kotera definitely came from the gun found at the scene."

"Mr. Spearling, as you are in charge of the Westchester County CSI unit, what else was in the report of the shooting?"

"Well, the investigation found that the owner of the gun was Joseph Blandenberg. He bought it in 2008 and registered it with the county. In other words, it was a legal gun but only licensed for home use, for protection."

"Anything else?"

"Yes, we tested the gun for finger prints and found that the only prints on the gun were that of Mr. Blandenberg. We also tested the defendant for gun powder residue and found that he had such residue on his hands and clothes that would indicate that he had fired a gun in the last eight hours or so."

"Thank you, Mr. Spearling, your witness Mr. Graham."

Jesse began his cross: "Mr. Spearling, you testified that your total experience in forensics and being a coroner is thirty-two years, and you've worked in Chicago, Baltimore and now Westchester County. That's correct, right?"

Spearling nodded and said: "yes."

"OK, in your vast experience how many shootings have you investigated, and I know you don't have an exact figure, so please just approximate."

"I couldn't possibly know off hand."

Jesse came back: "OK, is the number, say ten, twenty-five, or more?"

"Much more" responded Spearling.

"Could it be, maybe five hundred?"

"Yes, it could be."

"OK, here's my question. Based on your vast experience doing investigations of shootings, how often were there felony shootings in which a 22 caliber gun was used? Give me an answer like, frequently, about 50% of the time, or rarely."

Spearling responded: "Rarely."

"And why is that, in your professional opinion?"

"Well, most likely because the 22 has very little firing power. It uses a small bullet."

Jesse then asked: "How is it that this small bullet actually killed Mr. Kotera?"

Spearling answered: "The shot missed Mr. Kotera's rib cage and entered his abdomen. A few inches higher or to the right, then Mr. Kotera might have survived."

"What if Mr. Kotera had been wearing a coat?"

Spearling answered: "The bullet probably wouldn't have entered his body. Again, the gun is a small caliber weapon."

Jesse then added: "Would it fit neatly into a women's purse?"

Spearling responded: "Yes."

"OK, last question and again in your professional opinion, if Mr. Blandenberg was intent on murdering Mr. Kotera, wouldn't he have chosen a more powerful weapon? Again, in your professional opinion."

"Yes."

"No more questions for this witness."

Jesse was surprised that the prosecutor did not object even once during this cross-examination and whispered that to Joe after the testimony.

The trial was then recessed for lunch.

In the afternoon, Ms. Smith called several other witnesses to the stand. These witnesses were a professional psychologist and the other an expert witness in profiling who testified that there were thousands of boys just like Richard who would never consider harming anyone. The questioning went on for the remainder of the day.

That night, on Carter's Court, Jeanne Carter had a field day, ranting and raving, how Jesse was trying to persuade the jurors that his client had not intended to kill the boy, only maim him. She said this with total disdain. The other panelists, however, were not so strident in their comments. They felt that the defense had made some good points, especially about the 22 caliber gun. But, overall, the panel, as well as public opinion was still clearly against Joe.

Day four of the trial-

The day started with the testimony of Sharon Kotera. The prosecutor anticipated that Jesse would show that her son was not normal. In addition, Jesse might imply that she was negligent in not getting him help when he first needed it.

Sharon came across as a sympathetic witness. She gave a history of her life, with her husband leaving her and the boy many years ago. She said that she tried her best to give Richard a good home life. She said that she knew Richard was a loner, but still can't believe that he intended to harm anyone, as the defense has been charging. She cried several times during her testimony and had to compose herself. Her testimony for the prosecution lasted for almost five hours.

When Smith was finished with her, Jesse only asked her two questions. One had to do with the number of times she was called to the school to speak to a teacher or guidance counselor about Richard's behavior, and two, was she aware of what Richard was doing on the computer.

He was treating her with kid gloves as she had suffered the death of her only child and he didn't want to come across as a cold-hearted person.

When he was through with her, the trial adjourned until Monday morning when the defense would call its first witnesses. Over the weekend, Jesse, Jane and Joe's entire family visited him in jail.

Michael gave his dad some good news. Between everyone's assets and Jesse's contact with a bail bondsman from the city, Jesse would be able to make bail early next week.

After the family left, Jesse and Joe started to go over their defense witnesses. This is where Jesse would try to make the case that Joe knew in advance what Richard Kotera was planning. There would be at least three colleagues of Joe's from his days at the Defense Department, who would testify as to Joe's character as well as his abilities in the field of extra-sensory perception.

Then, the plan was to let Jane testify. She would tell what she saw at the Christmas dinner, when Joe read his son's mind about his job change. Then by Tuesday, the results of the examination of Richard's computer would be finished. The results would be reviewed and if they could help Joe, Jesse would ask the FBI technician to testify on his behalf.

The prosecution had maintained all along that there was nothing on the boy's computer that could help Joe. The Westchester CSI computer expert had gone over the contents of the computer, but this gentleman, as Jesse had found out was about fifty years old and Jesse was hoping that he missed something that the FBI lab would not.

Day five of the trial-

It was Monday and Jesse was ready to call his first witnesses. They were John Miller, Seth Bergen and Ben Jacobs, all retired Defense Department employees. Each of them described Joe's work at the DOD and that they had seen him show signs of ESP.

They also said that Joe was the "salt of the earth." Their testimonies and Smith's cross examinations took up most of the day. It was not very exciting and Jesse didn't think that the jury was persuaded that Joe's abilities were real.

By that evening, Jesse received the report from the FBI technician who had examined Richard's computer, and based on that report, Jesse asked the judge to issue a subpoena to confiscate another computer located at the high school.

Jesse then asked the judge to adjourn the trial until that second computer had been examined. The judge adjourned the trial until the following Monday. The prosecutor was not happy because the results of these tests would not be disclosed to her until just before presentation at the trial.

Meanwhile Joe was released on bail, and although led out of the jail by a back entrance he had to wade through an avalanche of reporters yelling questions to him. Joe's son and daughter were waiting for him in a hired car and took him straight to his son's apartment in the city.

The rest of his family was already there, along with Jane and Jesse. It was thought best not to bring him home in Jerusalem as the reporters were staked out there, and there could always be some nut who would like nothing better than to kill Joe to avenge Richard's death.

The second computer was picked up by the FBI technician on Wednesday and within twenty-four hours he had finished his work. He called Jesse and said that he could meet him on Thursday to discuss his findings. Jesse asked for a one day delay in their meeting.

On Friday, Jesse met with FBI computer technician Alan Green at Jesse's office downtown at Foley Square. Green presented Jesse with his written report and went through the contents of it, at length. At the conclusion of the presentation, Jesse asked if the agent would testify as to the contents of the report.

"Agent Green, I need you to testify as a defense witness."

Green replied: "I can only testify as to the contents of the report. You can call me as a witness but it will only be as a neutral scientist. I won't be labeled as a defense witness, but I will testify as to the contents of the two computers."

Jesse was satisfied and said that he would provide Agent Green with transportation to the Westchester court house on the following Monday.

Day six of the trial-

At 8 AM Monday, Jesse e-mailed the FBI report over to Barbara Smith. It was just two hours before the trial would resume and the prosecutor was not amused. There would be no time to read through the report before the agent testified.

When the trial resumed, Ms. Smith asked the judge for a one day continuance citing the tardiness in receiving the FBI report. The judge denied her request telling her that she was partly to blame since she had not turned over the computer much earlier in the process.

The judge said: "Mr. Martin, are you ready to call your next witness?"

"Yes, your honor, I call Alan Green." The agent took the oath and explained that he was an FBI lab technician that specialized in computer science. He was a graduate of Caltech and had a master's degree from Harvard. He had worked for the FBI for more than ten years.

Jesse asked: "Why with those credentials did you choose to work for the government when you could have had any job you wanted in the private sector?"

Green responded: "I guess it was because of 9-11. After seeing what happened that day, I decided I wanted to do something for my country. I didn't care about the money; I just wanted to do my part."

Then Jesse asked the agent to go through his report and that he, Jesse, would not interrupt.

Agent Green began: "I examined Mr. Kotera's computer hard drive, and all of the programs in it. At first, there was nothing extraordinary about what I had found. There were many programs, lots of files saved by the owner and not much else. I was looking for something but I wasn't sure what.

Your office asked me to look for anything having to do with violence, or plans to attack the school. I didn't find anything like that. After looking for about eight hours, I was about to give up. Then by accident, I clicked on the icon that says My Computer. When that opened, it showed the various drives on the computer, and the amount of memory on each drive."

Jesse said: "Continue, please."

Green resumed: "I knew that this particular Tri-Tech desktop computer was supposed to have a total of 8 gigabytes of memory. However, when I added up all of the memory either used or unused, the total only came up to 7.2 gigs. In other words, there were 800 megabytes of memory missing. I installed a program that would search for the missing memory."

Jesse: "What did you find?"

"Well, it was ingenious. Someone had installed a program that was invisible on the computer but had a very interesting and unusual purpose. Mr. Kotera could use that part of memory to surf the web for various sites that one didn't want others to know about. Similarly, he could chat with others and none of the conversations would be saved on the computer."

Jesse interrupted: "How is that possible?"

Green resumed: "Well, this program made it so that once it was activated by a user, any taps on the keyboard at home would not register on the computer but would, in fact, register on a remote computer."

Jesse asked: "Did you find where this second computer was located?"

"Yes, it was located in the computer sciences lab at JFK High School in Jerusalem New York. Once retrieved, I was able to see everything that the user did with his computer."

"Could you tell us what you found?"

"Yes, I'll go in order. First off, Mr. Kotera had visited on a daily basis, websites that glorified violence, Satan, guns, revenge and the like. The user spent about ten hours each week for over a year visiting these sites. Next we found that Mr. Kotera was conducting a long-term series of chats with a person located in Pasadena California. These chats went through a website named: The Legions of Lucifer.com."

Jesse asked: "What was the nature of that website?"

Mr. Green then said: "It is a website dedicated to extreme violence and sadism. There are computer games about mass killings, Satanism and chat rooms for people to communicate, all on that site. I Googled that name and found that there were attempts to have that site removed from the internet as it was way too violent."

At that point, Jesse introduced a transcript of these chats as defense exhibit 3. With the aid of a laptop computer and an overhead projector, the chats were shown in a PowerPoint format while at the same time being read out loud by a court officer.

From the look on the juror's faces, these chats were devastating to the prosecution for they clearly showed that Kotera was planning mass murder. There was no way around it. The reading of the chat dialog went on for about an hour before Jesse mercifully cut it short.

When it was finished, Jesse continued questioning agent Green.

"Now, Mr. Green, do you remember where you left off?"

"Yes, there was more. On March 27th and 28th Richard surfed the internet looking for ways to buy a gun. He found that there was going to be a gun show in Wayne New Jersey a few days later. There were also searches on the websites of gun manufacturers. He was apparently looking for the right gun at the right price. He spent the most time on the website of Glock Guns and Ammunition."

"Thank you Mr. Green"

The prosecutor was so flabbergasted by what everyone had just seen and heard, she had no questions for the FBI technician. She, herself now was harboring some doubts about Joe's guilt.

At that point, Judge Grobin was feeling a little under the weather so he adjourned the trial until the next day.

Back at Michael's apartment Jesse and the family discussed strategy for the next day. Jane was scheduled to testify, but Joe did not want her to look foolish on the stand discussing ESP. She also would have to face her peers at the college and he didn't want her to get hurt more than she already was. So Joe told Jesse that he wanted to testify on his own behalf.

Jesse said that this was very dangerous as he would also have to be grilled by Barbara Smith on cross-examination. Once he opened the door on his transient psychic powers, she would try to destroy whatever credibility he had earned during the trial.

Joe said that he didn't care. He wanted to tell his story. He had nothing to hide and nothing to be ashamed of. He never reveled in the fact that he killed Kotera but he did not shed a tear for the boy for he knew what he had planned.

Jesse continued to argue: "I have rarely if ever allowed any of my clients to testify on their own behalf. In your case, it won't do much good, unless of course you could read the minds of the jurors in front of the court. Yet I don't see that happening, do you?"

Joe responded: "I don't care. I know it's a crap shoot. Look, I'm probably going to prison. I don't want the world to remember me as a vicious killer of a young boy. I want to." Joe didn't finish his sentence and started to sob.

"OK Joe, it's your call in the end. Let's prepare for tomorrow. We'll go over the questions I will ask you and how you should answer them. I mean, I want you to use certain words and phrases. Of course you will tell the truth, but the way you express yourself will be very important. Also, when you answer the questions, look right at the jury. Don't look away. Looking away will imply that you have something to hide.

After I'm finished, the prosecutor will get her chance to question you. She will not be kind, I can assure you. She will try to get you flustered. She will ask rapid-fire questions hardly giving you a chance to answer. She wants you to make a mistake.

If she does that, do not answer. Wait about ten seconds and then ask her to repeat each question slowly, one at a time. Then answer each question slowly, again, looking directly at the jury."

Joe said that he understood. He would keep his cool under fire.

Jesse then added: "And yes, your ace in the hole, if by a miracle, you should start having your visions while I am questioning you, let me know by coughing three times. At that point, just follow my lead."

For the next two hours, Jesse went through the questions he would be asking Joe, and the answers he hoped to hear back. Then, they went through what Jesse said would be the prosecutor's cross-examination. Jesse played the role of Ms. Smith and for over an hour, asked the questions that tried to put Joe on the defensive. The questions were accusatory in nature but Joe held up pretty well, much to the satisfaction of Jesse.

That evening on Carter's Court, Jeanne Carter finally admitted that there may have been something wrong with Richard Kotera. The FBI agent's testimony was eye-opening. The other regular panelists on the show agreed and one boldly stated that Joe may be found innocent.

The public is quite sick over all of the recent school shootings and it wants those to stop. Maybe the cause is too many guns, maybe it's short-comings in the mental health area or maybe it's all the violent movies and video games, but if a shooting can be prevented in any way, the public would be all for that.

Even with the shocking testimony about Richard, Jeanne still predicted that Joe would be found guilty. She always has the final word on her show.

Chapter Ten

Day seven of the trial-

The judge said: "Mr. Graham, please call your first witness."

Jesse had notified the prosecutor that he would be changing the order of witnesses, having Joe testify now and delaying Jane until after.

Jesse responded: "I call Joseph Blandenberg."

The court officer asked: "Do you swear to tell the truth, the whole truth and nothing but the truth, so help you God?" Joe answered: "I do."

"Please state your name and address for the court."

Joe answered and waited for Jesse to ask his first question.

"Joe, did you shoot Richard Kotera on the morning of May 23, 2012?"

Jesse answered: "Yes." There was a noticeable gasp in the court room. Jesse waited a moment and then asked: "Could you tell the court why you did this?"

"Yes." and after a long pause continued: "Mr. Kotera was on his way to his high school that morning, and he was going to commit mass murder of his fellow students and teachers. I felt that since I was sure this was going to happen, it was my civic duty, my moral duty, to stop him."

Jesse then asked: "What was going through your mind at the time you confronted him near his home that morning?"

"I was walking toward his street when he approached the intersection. I asked him for his name, to make sure he was the right person, the one I had met before. When he confirmed that he was Richard, I shot him."

"Was it your intention to kill him?"

"No, I just wanted to stop him. It wasn't in my mind that I had to kill him. I figured that if I just shot him, there would be an investigation, and questions would be asked about the weapons he was carrying, and his motives. However, I have to admit that if he died, I knew that he would never be able to plan another atrocity. That's why I shot him in the stomach, and not in a leg. It's like you're damned if you do and damned if you don't." As Joe was speaking, he made sure that he was looking straight at the jury, just as he was told to.

Jesse knew that if he didn't ask these questions, the prosecutor would. Admitting to the shooting right up front might work to Joe's advantage showing that he had nothing to hide.

Jesse then said: "OK, now that we have that out of the way, please tell about yourself, and your family. First, tell the court about your work for the federal government."

Joe began his story: "I worked for the US government in the Department of Defense for about twenty-five years from 1983 to the end of 2008. After spending eight years as a US Marine, I worked for the DOD's Psychological Warfare Division. My job was to perfect or enhance, if possible, extra-sensory perception for our intelligence officers during the latter part of the Cold War. I was in charge of many projects for the government.

We conducted many tests on whether humans could use ESP as either a weapon, or as an intelligence gathering method. These would be conducted similar to how drug trials are conducted by the pharmaceutical industry."

"What were the results of these tests and trials?"

"In my opinion, they were all successful and we were making great progress in understanding ESP and how what parts of the brain controlled it."

Jesse then asked: "Isn't it so that the government was not overjoyed with your progress and reduced your budgets each year?"

"Yes, that's true. However, we were always dealing with bureaucrats and pencil pushers. Even the generals lost interest after the Cold War was over and our government started to reduce the defense budgets in the mid-to-late nineties."

"Is that why you retired from government service?"

71

"That's part of it. In 2005 my wife was diagnosed with cancer. By late 2008, she needed me to help her cope with the fact that she was going to die. I left my job to be with her in her last year of life. However, this coincided with a down-sizing of many programs of the Defense Department.

My department was part of the down-sizing. I was offered a buy-out, so to speak. I could retire then, at the age of 53 and even though I only had thirty-three years of government service, including my years in the Marines.

I would be credited with forty years of service. However, the trade-off was that I couldn't start collecting my pension until I was fifty-five. It was a good deal for me because my pension would be $85,000 per year and that would assure my financial future."
Jesse next asked: "OK Joe, how did you get your last position at Moab College?"

Joe answered: "A position opened up due to a teacher's death, coincidentally, in the Psychology Department of the college in April 2012. I applied for the job and was accepted."

Jesse said: "Go on please."

Joe then added: "The subject was Psychology One, which was the basic starter course in the subject. I had to teach several one hour classes each week and give one two-hour lecture. The lectures were always filled to capacity because that was where the students and I spoke about ESP.

Some of these students testified earlier. Almost every one of these students has some degree of ESP and they wanted to know why that was so. They also were hoping to enhance their abilities. These students were true believers in that science."

Joe: "What actually got you into this field?"

Joe answered: "Because I have these abilities. I've had them all of my life, but they ebb and flow, like the tides."

"Joe, could you tell the court how you knew that Richard Kotera was planning mass murder that 23rd day in May, 2012?"

"Because I read his mind."
"When was that, the day of the shooting?"

"No, it started several months before. We were both walking to our respective schools, when we almost had a collision. The near collision was his fault but he did not acknowledge me. I stared at him and said something; I don't remember the exact words. He didn't say anything but I could hear his thoughts and know that he was thinking of killing his tormentors. Those were the words I heard. I know it sounds crazy but it's true."

All the while, Joe was looking straight at the jurors.

Jesse then said: "Why should anyone believe you?"

Joe, again looking straight at the jurors said: "Because it's the truth. Hasn't everyone had some sort of episode where maybe they were thinking of some one, and an instant later the phone rang and it was that person?

Or, hasn't someone had a feeling of déjà vu where one feels a sensation that an event or experience currently being experienced had also been experienced in the past?"

Joe continued: "My feelings at that time were so strong that I made it my mission to watch this boy over the next few months. I walked the same route, hoping to meet up with him again. Each time I did, I felt nothing. It was as if Mr. Kotera was masking his feelings, or maybe he was thinking of other things.

Finally, two days before the planned shooting, I saw him, walked close to him and felt the most horrible feelings in my life. I then knew what he was planning and when."

Jesse's questions and Joe's testimony went on for the rest of the day. When he was finished, he requested the right, if necessary, to ask additional questions on re-direct after the prosecutor's cross examination.

The trial was adjourned until the next day. After it was over, Joe was spent. He didn't want to make the long trip back to New York, so he and the rest of the family and the defense team went back to Joe's house for the night.

By this time, most of the roving reporters had left. A police car was parked in front of the house with two officers inside.

Jesse told Joe that he had done very well. A jury consultant who had been hired by Jesse reported that eight of the jurors looked very sympathetic to the defense arguments. She couldn't tell about the other four. However, no one really knows how a juror will vote when in deliberations.

Joe was very tired and went to bed at 9 PM. The next day in court might be decisive. If he could survive the prosecutor's barrage of questions without losing his cool, he might have a good chance of being found not guilty.

When the trial first started, Joe felt that there wasn't a chance in hell that he could be exonerated. But now, after Jesse's great defense, he felt cautiously optimistic.

Jesse described his strategy as jury nullification. That's where an attempt is made to convince a jury to find a defendant not guilty, even though he is technically guilty of committing the crime.

In any case, the entire household went to bed very nervous about the next day.

Chapter Eleven

Day eight of the trial-

The court convened promptly at 10 AM. The court was packed to standing room only. As Judge Grobin entered, everyone stood up.

"Be seated everyone" Grobin stated.

"Ms. Smith, do you wish to cross-examine the last witness, the defendant?"

"Yes, your honor."

Joe was asked back to the witness box. The judge reminded him that he was still under oath.

The prosecutor asked a series of questions concerning Joe's career and family life. These lasted for about an hour and seemed to be setting the stage for the hard questions to come.

Finally, Ms. Smith asked: "Mr. Blandenberg, you testified that your first encounter with Richard was in January 2012. Isn't that so?"

"Yes."

"You also admit to shooting him on May 23rd, right?"

"Yes, that's correct."

"So, for almost five months you stalked him, until you decided to kill him."

Joe responded: "I wouldn't go that far. I wasn't stalking him. I was just trying to meet up with him to verify what I believed after my first encounter with him."

Smith countered: "I don't know. It sure seems like you were stalking him. You walked past his route almost every day and followed him to his house to get his address. What would you call that?"

Jesse shouted out: "Objection, the witness already answered that."

The judge overruled the objection and let Smith continue.

"Mr. Blandenberg, in all your years investigating the phenomenon of ESP you stated that you have the power to read one's mind. Have you ever had the experience of being wrong?"

"Truthfully, yes. I've been wrong on several occasions."

"So, how were you so sure about your conclusions about Richard Kotera? Isn't it possible you were wrong then? And why, if you could be wrong, would you shoot the poor boy? Isn't that so final?

"Objection, the DA is badgering the witness."

Ms. Smith, will you let the witness answer each question before you ask another?"

"Sorry, your honor"

"Mr. Blandenberg, I'm thinking of a number between one and ten. Can you tell me what it is?"

Joe answered: "No, I can't, it doesn't work that way."

"Well, what way does it work?"

Joe responded: "I just can't turn it on and off. I would get the feeling all of a sudden, and then I would be able to do it."

"Do what, Mr. Blandenberg?"

"You know, read ones mind."

Ms. Smith started to snicker and said: "Are you joking? You must take everyone here for a fool." As she said that she walked from the microphone and toward the witness box until she was about three feet away from Joe.

Smith was now speaking in a very loud voice "Isn't it true that you are a liar? You really don't have any power to read a mind. You never read Richard's mind. You were just fixated on him for some reason, stalked him and shot him for no valid reason."

At this point, Joe was agitated and shaking. Jesse stood up and objected and the judge sustained the objection asking Smith once again to stop badgering the witness.

Next, Ms. Smith asked Joe when he first noticed that he had ESP. Joe said that he couldn't remember but that it was a long time ago when he was a teenager. Smith then asked Joe to relate some of these experiences from the past.

Joe said that he couldn't remember things that happened many years ago. These feelings came and went, and very infrequently. He could only remember the recent event at his house last Christmas when he read his son's mind about the new job.

"You have got to be kidding. You tell this court that you have ESP but can only remember one episode. Again you must think we are all fools." The prosecutor again began to harangue Joe, trying to get him to admit that he was a liar.

All of a sudden, Joe looked at Jesse and started to cough. He coughed three times and the judge asked him if he was OK.

"Yes, your honor."

Judge Grobin than said to Smith: "You've been at this for over an hour and you seem to be re-hashing the same questions over and over. Do you have any further questions for the witness?

"No, your honor, I think we've all seen enough of this witness."

Jesse stood up and asked the judge for permission to ask more questions under re-direct. The judge granted his request.

Immediately, Jesse asked his first question: "Joe, you testified that your power to read a mind is transitory and can come and go at any time. You cannot control when you have the power, right?"

"Yes."

"Joe, can you read my mind right now?"

Joe was looking at the jury and answered yes.

Joe paused for a few seconds and looked right at the judge and asked if he could say something to him. The judge agreed.

"Your honor, you have been thinking of your daughter. I know that she went to the doctor for a test last week and you had been worried about her. You've had a weight lifted off you as the tumor was benign."

The judge looked quizingly at Joe and said: "What did you say?"

"I said that" the judge stopped him in mid-sentence. "I heard you, Mr. Blandenberg."

"Joe, do you know what the jury foreperson is thinking right now?" asked Jesse.

Smith stood up and objected. She said: "Your honor, Mr. Graham is trying to turn this proceeding into a circus. This is ridiculous and I request that he be forbidden to continue with this charade."

"Mr. Graham, what say you?" asked the judge.

"Your honor, it seems to me that we are at the crux of this case. If Mr. Blandenberg is psychic and can read minds, then he is not guilty. If he can prove that to the jurors then they cannot in good conscience, find him guilty. So, I request that you give the defendant his chance to prove that he has the ability to read minds."

The judge, still in shock over Joe's comments to him agreed. He said: "OK, Mr. Graham, I'm giving you some latitude here but don't make this a circus."

Grobin spoke to the jury: "To the members of the jury, we will be doing a little experiment. The defendant will ask each of you, starting with the foreperson, to think of something, anything. He will then attempt to tell the court what you were thinking of. There is no need to respond. Only you will know if the defendant was correct.

However, you will ignore Mr. Graham's statement that if the defendant can read minds, then he is not guilty. You will decide that only after the trial is over and after you have deliberated over all of the evidence."

"OK Mr. Graham, you can proceed"

"Joe, are you ready?" I'm going to ask each member of the jury, one at a time to think of anything that comes to their minds. Madam foreperson, you are first. Please look at the defendant and think of anything."

Joe looked at her for about fifteen seconds and said: "Ma'am, you are thinking that you cannot wait for this trial to be over so that you and your family can go on your vacation to California."

The lady looked at Joe and smiled.

Jesse then asked the man to her left to do the same thing.

Joe looked right at him and within a few seconds said: "You are thinking whether the New York Yankees will win the World Series this year. To tell you the truth, I'm wondering that myself."

The man started to laugh. You could see the prosecutor sinking into her chair. Then Jesse asked the next woman juror to do the same thing.

Joe said to her: "I don't know if I should say this (the woman started to smile) but you want to know if I sleep in my pajamas or in the nude. There, I said it."

Jesse continued with the rest of the jurors, one by one, and Joe read their minds perfectly. When he got to the final juror, Jesse asked the woman to pick a number between one and one hundred.

Joe exclaimed: "fifty five." The juror just shook her head in amazement.

Then Joe looked at Ms. Smith for a few seconds and without being prompted, said to her: "Ms. Smith, yes, your case "is" falling apart." Smith stared at him without making a comment."

Jesse looked at the judge and said: "Your honor, the defense rests."

The judge said that the trial would resume in the morning for closing statements and the court room emptied slowly. Joe's family and Jane rushed to his side and each started to hug him.

Jesse said: "Hey, the trial isn't over so let's not get ahead of ourselves here. Let's head on back to the house and discuss my closing statement for tomorrow.

Back at the house, Jesse congratulated Joe on his performance that afternoon. He asked: "What happened?"

Joe said: "I'm not sure, but when Smith was pressuring me and calling me a liar, my emotions got the better of me, I guess. All of a sudden, I could hear lots of thoughts moving around my head.

The first one I could make out was Judge Grobin's, possibly because he was closest to me. I don't know, it just came to me."

"Yeah, just in the nick of time. What about now?" Jesse asked.

"I've got nothing. It's gone. I hope I don't have to give another demonstration anytime soon."

"Don't worry, I don't think so."

Chapter Twelve

Day nine of the trial-

The court room filled quickly. There was a huge crowd outside that couldn't get in. Even Jeanne Carter and her minions were there. It was certainly a circus atmosphere, one that the judge wanted to avoid. However, all of the participants were now TV personalities. All of the main protagonists were smartly dressed and ready to do battle.

Carter's Court was being televised live from the court house. The county had provided a corner where Jeanne and her guest could set up. The panel discussed the prior day of court room drama. Carter had by now, softened her view of the defendant.

Jeanne started speaking: "Good morning ladies and gentlemen. Today we will hear closing arguments in the Joseph Blandenberg murder trial. Yesterday, the trial was full of drama where it appeared that the defendant was given wide latitude by the judge to try to prove that he was a mind reader.

It was, to say, interesting, if not ridiculous. Blandenberg was purportedly reading each juror's thoughts. However, the judge instructed the jurors not to reveal whether Blandenberg was correct. So, only the jurors know for sure. We watched as each juror was polled, so to speak, and it appeared that each of them found Blandenberg's answers amusing."

Jeanne's guests for the day were Jim Cortland and J.T. Sanderford, both renowned defense attorneys. Both of them complimented Jesse Graham's defense of Joe Blandenberg. They agreed that even without the final histrionics, Graham had provided a masterful defense.

Cortland responded to Jeanne: "But the testimony about Richard's secret computer chats over the web seems to have provided the jury with an escape clause to not find him guilty of murder. I think that Blandenberg was over-charged from the get go. Jesse's attempts at jury nullification are working, in my opinion."

Sanderford agreed: "That, plus the fact that the boy was carrying a loaded Glock 51 with three more clips of ammunition was enough to scare the "be Jesus" out of any sane person."

Jeanne of course had the last word.

"Well it may all come down to the summations by the lawyers. If Jesse can convince even one juror to acquit, we'll have a hung jury. I don't see Blandenberg beating the charges but a hung jury may result in a re-trial with reduced charges. Anyway, we'll know in a few days, I suppose."

The court was in order when the judge told Barbara Smith to begin her summation.

Barbara got up off her chair and approached to within a few feet of the jury box.

"Ladies and gentlemen of the jury, you are here to decide the guilt or innocence of Joseph Blandenberg. I would like to go through some of the evidence that you have heard and seen over the last two weeks or so. Once you review these, this becomes a very easy case to adjudicate.

The defendant, Joseph Blandenberg, on a warm May morning walked up to the deceased, Richard Kotera, and shot him in cold blood. He then called 911 and waited for the police to arrive. He dropped his gun, and sat, not five feet from Richard's dead body and waited. When the authorities arrived, he did not shed a tear. He was cold, and matter of fact.

He had been stalking the boy for several months, and finally, on May 23, 2013, murdered Richard. How do we know all of this? We know it because Mr. Blandenberg admitted it in open court just a few days ago.

This should be an open and shut case but the defense has muddied the waters with theories and court room histrionics that were designed to steer you away from the facts.

The defendant says that he read Richard's mind, and that Richard was planning to commit mass murder. How do we actually know that? I don't know. The defendant wants us to take it at faith that he is telling the truth, and that he could not have been mistaken.

In his first encounter with Richard, the defendant said that he felt bad vibes. Bad vibes, what are those. He did not understand them, but he had made up his mind that this boy was no good.

He claims that later, he knew that Richard was going to kill his fellow students at his high school, all because he read Richard's mind. How did the defendant know that Richard was really going to commit this terrible act? He could have been mistaken.

He admitted in court that he has made mistakes before, in this mind reading game of his. He could have been mistaken. Has anyone here ever had bad thought about something or someone? I know that I have. There have been times that I have imagined someone dead for some wrong that they had done to me. Now, I didn't really mean it. I never would have killed anyone because I, along with almost everyone else in America am a law-abiding citizen. Isn't it possible that Richard, in a bad mood, was thinking, just thinking, of murdering his tormentors at school?

And, just at that moment, the defendant comes along. Richard might not have actually gone through with it. Think about it, it could have been you. And what if some one-man vigilante squad decides that, based on what he heard in your mind, that one time, you had to be killed.

Here in America we have the rule of law. The defendant went to the police with flimsy evidence, or rather no evidence that Richard was planning murder. But when the police did not take him seriously, he decided to take the law into his own hands. We can't have that in America. If we did, we'd have chaos, and anarchy.

The bottom line here is that we have a man admitting that he killed an eighteen-year old boy in cold blood, without warning and with malice. There is really nothing else to consider. The defense would like you to acquit the defendant even though he has admitted to the crime. It claims to have mitigating circumstances. Those circumstances are dubious, at best.

I want you to go and fairly deliberate, because the law says that the defendant deserves a fair trial. However you must not allow the defense to get away with murder. Do not let Joe Blandenberg get away with murder."

A large number of people sitting in the court room gallery started to clap loudly. It was a short, but magnificent summation, considering that the defense now had an up-hill battle to win. The judge had to bang his gavel to restore order.

Judge Grobin then waved to Jesse: Mr. Graham, Your final arguments please."

"Ladies and gentlemen of the jury, I believe that the defendant, Joseph Blandenberg has proved that he is not a murderer. A killer, yes but not a murderer. There is a big difference between the two. Under the law, a murderer is a person who causes the death of another human being with malice. In this case, there is no proof of malice. Let me show you the difference. But let me preface this by stating that absent criminal insanity people committing the following would be considered murderers.

The ones who went on the rampages at schools in Columbine, at Virginia Tech, at Newtown, and at a theater in Aurora Colorado, and killed scores of children and teachers, those people are murderers. And a person who kills another while committing a violent felony such as armed robbery, that person is a murderer.

However, a person who kills another person in self-defense is not a murderer. A soldier who kills an enemy soldier in combat is not a murderer and a person who accidentally kills another during a fist fight is also not a murderer. I also maintain that a person, who kills another because he had prior knowledge that a mass killing will take place at the hands of the latter, is also not a murderer. Some might say he is a hero.

Joe was a happy, law-abiding citizen of Jerusalem, New York but because of a chance encounter with Mr. Kotera, faced a huge dilemma. If he did nothing about what he knew, possibly dozens of children would have lost their lives at the hands of this deranged man.

As you have heard, Joe was a US Marine for eight years and then an employee of the Department of Defense for another twenty-five. After retirement, he found another calling and was teaching at Moab College before his life was unalterably changed.

Many witnesses have come forward and testified to Joe's good character. None have done so for the victim, not even his mother. He was a troubled boy, a loner, no friends, a non-participant in every aspect of life. His father had left the home when he was five and for him, it was down-hill from that point on. As you have heard, he frequented the most horrible and violent websites on the internet and chatted with others, particularly a like-minded person who lived in California. Such is the nature of modern communications.

Mr. Kotera was also devious. You heard from the FBI's analysis that Mr. Kotera tried to hide his internet activities from the world. And, he almost got away with it. You heard the transcripts of those chats. They were enough to make one sick.

The prosecutor has tried to demonize the defendant and describe Mr. Kotera as a poor victim, a mere boy. Some boy!!! He was old enough to go to a Wayne, New Jersey gun show and buy a Glock 31 semi-automatic hand-gun. A bullet from that gun would literally blow your head off. This was no boy, this was a man. A guaranteed mass-murderer if my client did not stop him.

Now, let's compare ammunition. My client went to the scene of the crime with a 22 caliber hand-gun. The medical examiner testified that this type of weapon would not be the choice of a person intent on murdering another. What were his exact words? Oh yes, this gun could fit into a woman's purse.

You heard Joe state that his intent was not to kill Mr. Kotera but only to stop him. On the other hand, Mr. Kotera came to the confrontation with a Glock 31. That is a 357 Magnum, the weapon of choice of hired killers, police departments and military personnel. The gun was fully loaded and he was carrying three extra clips of ammunition. What does that tell you?

You heard testimony from Joe's fellow employees from the government that Joe had the gift of ESP. You heard his students testifying about his lectures. I always felt that if Joe could prove that he could read minds, he would be exonerated of this crime.

For months I asked Joe to concentrate, or get himself into a trance, or something, so that he could prove to me that he was psychic. But, as he said to the court, this power would come and go, and Joe had no control over it.

So, when Ms. Smith cross-examined him on the stand, Joe indicated to me that this feeling had come back to him, right then and there. That's why we asked to do the experiment where you would think of something, and Joe would tell you what it was. Now, no one knows if Joe was correct, except each of you.

When you go in to deliberate, you should ask each other whether Joe was correct. The bottom line of this case is if Joe proved to you that he did read your minds, he was not lying when he said he had read Mr. Kotera's.

Lastly, the prosecutor told you that in our society, we can't have people taking the law into their own hands or else we will have chaos. Well, I believe that you will agree that Joe's actions were not chaos but prevented such. Put yourselves in Joe's shoes. What would you have done?

Think about all of those children he saved. What if someone knew, in advance what Hitler was planning. Wouldn't killing him have been the right thing to do? I think so. So, ladies and gentlemen, I ask you to be fair, and find Joe Blandenberg, not guilty. It's the moral thing to do."

As Jesse completed his summation, the crowd in the court room exploded into cheering and clapping. It took several minutes to restore order. It was lunchtime. Judge Grobin ordered the jurors to go deliberate in one of the five conference rooms. Lunch would be brought to them.

He adjourned the court but reminded the jurors that they would be forbidden to discuss the case with anyone other than themselves.

The opposing parties walked out of the court room to a throng of reporters, well-wishers and the general public. Jesse Graham and Barbara Smith were standing within fifteen feet of each other. They both were answering questions from the media. There was much noise, everyone talking over everyone else.

This was the true media circus that everyone predicted. The warring attorneys answered every question as if they were spin doctors for a political candidate. Neither side would win this war. The real war would be in the deliberations room.

Chapter Thirteen

Joe, his family, Jane and his legal team went back to the house in Jerusalem to wait out the verdict. They were home by 3 PM. Two hours later, Joe asked Jesse how long it might take for the jury to come to a verdict. Jesse couldn't answer him.

"You never know. Every case is different." The hours went by without hearing from the judge. By 11 PM, all went to bed, and hoped that the morning would bring good news.

However, the next morning came and went and still there was no word. Jane was flipping out. It looked like she was having a nervous breakdown. Jesse's secretary called the doctor and, he agreed to make a rare house call after his office was closed.

He arrived by six o'clock that evening with valium in hand and told Jane to take one pill that night, and one each day thereafter for a week. Within an hour, she was asleep. The jury was now out for more than a day.

Joe asked Jesse what that could mean.

"Joe, again, it's hard to tell. However, it's evident that the jurors are doing their jobs. When I defended Anton

Cruzillo, the person known as the Midtown Rapist, the jury was out four days, and he was found not guilty. So, don't worry yourself sick."

The jury was now out for two days. Joe was restless and pacing the rooms of his house. Everyone else was watching television trying not to think of the situation. All of a sudden, the telephone rang. It was James Matheson, the Westchester District Attorney. Jesse got on the phone.

"Jesse, we'd like you to come in, along with your client. We'd like to discuss a possible plea."

"Hold on, I'll tell my client." Jesse muffled the phone and told Joe who was on the other end and what the call was about. After a quick discussion, Joe agreed.

"Jim, what time would you like to meet?"

"Jesse, we have to do it right away. If the jury comes back before we complete the deal, all bets are off. I'm at the court house, in my office. Get here as soon as you can."

"OK, we'll be there in fifteen minutes."

The drive didn't take long and when they got there, they found that the jury was still out. They were ushered into Matheson's office. Barbara Smith was there, along with another ADA.

The DA spoke first: "Joe, I don't know how long the jury will take, nor do I know how it will rule, but we have a proposal for you. First, I have gone over all of the testimony, and I will say to you that I don't think that you are a cold-blooded killer. But, you did shoot that boy.

However, as Barbara pointed out in her summation, we can't have people shooting other people at will, just because they have a vision, or even if they have physical proof that a crime is about to be committed. We really believe in that philosophy, and we'd rather bring a case like this to trial, and lose it, rather than allowing one to go Scot-free without any repercussions.

Having said all that, we think that it may be time to settle this case with what we call a plea bargain. Look, you may be acquitted or you may be found guilty. No one will know until the jury comes back. It's a crap-shoot for both sides. Does either of us want to roll the dice?"

Matheson paused for a few seconds. "I will let Barbara give you the details of what we feel is fair. Barbara."

"Joe, we propose that you plead guilty to 3rd degree manslaughter. You will agree to serve one year in a minimum-security jail and you will receive credit for time served. After serving your jail time, you will be on probation for four more years.

You will have to turn in your guns and promise never to own one again. This is a one-time offer. If you reject it, we're prepared to accept the ruling of the jury, whichever way it goes."

"Jesse, what do you think?" asked Joe.

"Joe, I actually think that you will be acquitted, but there is always the possibility that you will spend the next twenty-five years in jail." You know, in the legal profession there are what we call the hazards of litigation. One of the hazards is that you can lose. I recommend that you take the deal offered. You'll serve some more time and then have the rest of your life to look forward to."

Joe looked at Jane, and she nodded. The rest of the family agreed that this plea-bargain would end the ordeal, so without further delay Joe said yes.

The family members hugged each other and tears flowed down everyone's cheeks.

There was some paper work to complete and then Matheson called Judge Grobin to tell him that a plea deal had been worked out. The judge would have to agree with the deal but that was usually a formality.

Ten minutes after the deal was signed, and unbeknownst to the parties, the jury had reached a verdict.

Two hours later, at around 4 PM, the court re-convened and the jury was led back in.

Judge Grobin began: "Ladies and gentlemen of the jury, the District Attorney and the defense have agreed to a plea bargain." There was an audible moan in the court room.

"This court wants to thank you for your hard work and diligent service. Your time in deliberations was not wasted time I assure you. However, you are now excused from service."

The jury members were led out of the room and left the building from the garage.

Judge Grobin asked Ms. Smith to announce the plea deal. Ms. Smith stood up and said: "Your honor, the prosecution and the defendant have agreed to a plea bargain. The defendant will plead guilty to 3rd degree manslaughter and serve a sentence of one to five years with the last four years suspended. We ask you to approve the deal."

Grobin responded: "I will accept the deal. We will adjourn until 10 AM tomorrow for sentencing. The trial was over and Joe and his family hugged each other and all started to cry. Sharon Kotera, who had been at the trial, throughout, was also crying.

That evening, four of the jurors appeared on Carter's Court. Jeanne Carter asked the foreperson: "Everyone in America who has had an interest in this case wants to know the answer to the 64 thousand dollar question. What was the verdict as decided by the jury?"

The foreperson, Judith Adler responded: "The jury voted to...........

www.ingramcontent.com/pod-product-compliance
Lightning Source LLC
Chambersburg PA
CBHW071627140626
46555CB00021B/1243